The Lion Who Saw Himself in the Water

For my family and loved one,
with love and thanks. – I.R.

First Edition 1998
Paperback Edition 2001

Published by Hoopoe Books,
a division of The Institute for the Study of Human Knowledge

The Library of Congress has catalogued the hardcover edition as follows:

Shah, Idries, 1924-
The lion who saw himself in the water / by Idries Shah : illustrated by Ingrid Rodriguez.
p. cm.
Summary: As he gapes and growls at his ferocious reflection in a pool of water as shiny as a mirror, a terrified lion grows desperately thirsty.
ISBN 1-883536-12-X (hdbk.)
[1. Folklore.] I. Rodriguez, Ingrid, ill. II. Title.
PZ8.1.S47Li 1997
398.24'529757—dc21 97-5170
[E] CIP
AC

The Lion Who Saw Himself in the Water

by Idries Shah

HOOPOE BOOKS
BOSTON

Now, once upon a time there was a lion and his name was Share the Lion. And he was king of all the animals in the jungle.

He had a lovely golden mane on his head, all furry — just like hair, only furry and golden. And he had a lovely golden coat. He used to go about and say "Grrrrrrrrrrrr" because that's how lions talk.

But not all the animals knew that he talked like that. And some of them, when they heard him say "Grrrrrrrrrrrr," were a little frightened, and they ran away.

And soon, because they saw some of their animal friends running, all the animals got a bit frightened, and they all started to run away.

Now, Share the Lion thought, "That's funny! Why is everybody running away from me?" So he shouted, "Grr-grrr?" which, in lion-talk, means "Why are you running away?"

Well, as we know, the other animals didn't understand lion-talk, and since he was by this time shouting very loudly, they all said, "Share the Lion, King of the Jungle, must be very, very angry with us now!" And so they ran even faster.

Of course, Share wasn't angry at all. He just wanted to know why they were all running away.

Then he thought, "Well, they are a silly lot of animals! I won't take any notice of them. I'm thirsty. I think I'll go and have a drink of water from a pool."

And he looked all over the place until he found some water.

Deep in the jungle there was a pool of water, and it was smooth and clear and shining just like a mirror. Share the Lion was now quite thirsty and, as he went near to it, he said to himself, "GRRRAR! I want a drink of waterrrr-grrr." That's how lions talk.

But as he leaned towards the water, which was shining like a mirror, he looked in and saw his own face reflected on the surface.

Well, he had never seen that before, and so he thought there was another lion in the pool of water, who was looking back at him.

And he was too afraid of this other lion to drink anything at all!

Wasn't he a funny lion?

"Oh, dear me!" he said to himself. "That's another lion, and he wants to stop me drinking his water." And then he said, "Grrrr!" to the other lion, which, in lion-talk, means "I want some water too!"

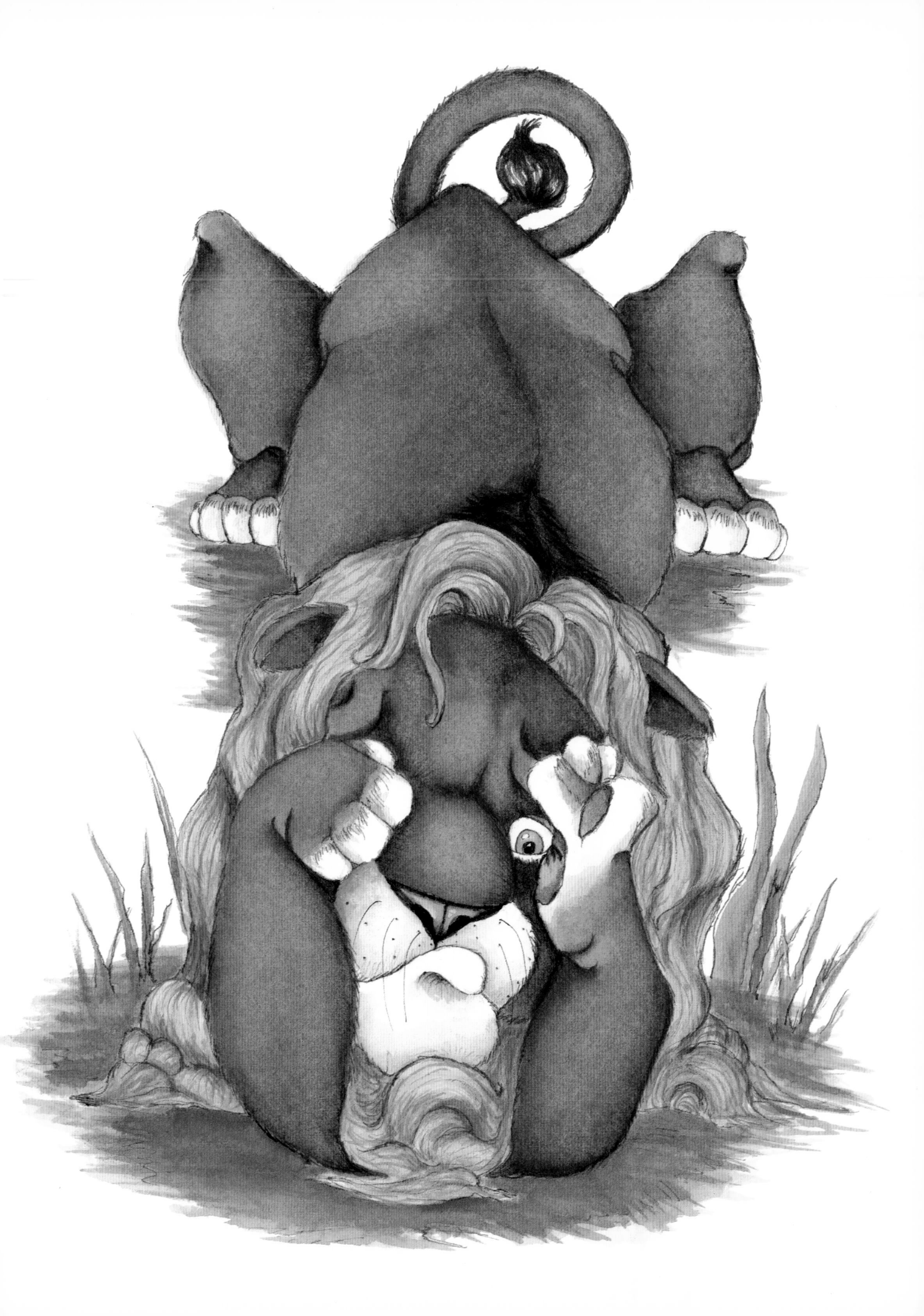

And then the other animals, who were now thirsty, came to drink water from the shining pool, and they saw Share the Lion and said, "What are you doing looking into the water and going 'Grr-grr' and not having a drink?"

Share the Lion sighed and said, "I can't have a drink of water because there is another lion in there, and he keeps saying 'Grr-grr' to me."

Some of the animals began to laugh a little when they heard him say this because they knew that it was his reflection in the water.

But Share the Lion didn't.

And then a beautiful butterfly flew very close to the Lion's ear and said in her tiny little voice, "Don't be silly, Share the Lion. There's nobody in the water!"

But Share the Lion said, "Of course there's somebody in the water. I can see him!"

And everybody just stopped and
waited to see what would happen.

And Share the Lion, King of the Jungle, got thirstier and thirstier and thirstier and thirstier, and in the end he said, "I don't care. I've got to have water. I am terribly thirsty. I don't care about that lion in there, or how fierce he is!"

And he put his head into the water, and when he did, he felt the lovely cool water in his mouth and began to drink. As he drank, he saw that the other lion had disappeared. Of course, it had disappeared because it was never really there at all. It was just his own reflection in the water.

And when he took his head out of the water and saw all the animals standing there, he said,"Well, at last I've learned that a reflection is not the same as the real thing!"

And so, everybody lived happily ever after.

Other Books by Idries Shah

For Young Readers
The Farmer's Wife
Neem the Half-Boy
The Magic Horse
The Silly Chicken
The Boy Without A Name
The Clever Boy and the Terrible, Dangerous Animal
World Tales

Literature
The Hundred Tales of Wisdom
A Perfumed Scorpion
Caravan of Dreams
Wisdom of the Idiots
The Magic Monastery
The Dermis Probe

Novel
Kara Kush

Informal Beliefs
Oriental Magic
The Secret Lore of Magic

Humor
The Exploits of the Incomparable Mulla Nasrudin
The Pleasantries of the Incredible Mulla Nasrudin
The Subtleties of the Inimitable Mulla Nasrudin
Special Illumination

Travel
Destination Mecca

Human Thought
Learning How to Learn
The Elephant in the Dark
Thinkers of the East
Reflections
A Veiled Gazelle
Seeker After Truth

Sufi Studies
The Sufis
The Way of the Sufi
Tales of the Dervishes
The Book of the Book
Neglected Aspects of Sufi Study
The Commanding Self